A DORLING KINDERSLEY BOOK

Written by Angela Royston
Photography by Dave King
Additional photography Tim Ridley (pages 4–5 and 8–9)
Illustrations by Jane Cradock-Watson and Dave Hopkins
Train consultant Julian Holland
Train models supplied by Victor's, London, and Beatties of London

LITTLE SIMON MERCHANDISE
An imprint of Simon & Schuster Children's Publishing Division
1230 Avenue of the Americas
New York, New York 10020

Eye Openers™
First published in Great Britain in 1992
by Dorling Kindersley Limited,
9 Henrietta Street, London WC2E 8PS

Reproduced by Colourscan, Singapore
Printed and bound in Italy by L.E.G.O., Vicenza

3 4 5 6 7 8 9 10

Trains.
p.   cm. — (Eye openers)
    "A Dorling Kindersley Book" — T.p. verso
    Summary: A simple introduction to different
types of freight and commuter trains.
    ISBN 0-689-71647-8
    1. Railroads—Juvenile literature.   [1. Railroads—Trains.]
I. King, Dave, ill.   II. Cradock-Watson, Jane, ill.
III. Hopkins, Dave, ill.   IV. Series.
TF148.T77 1992
625.1—dc20   92-12551

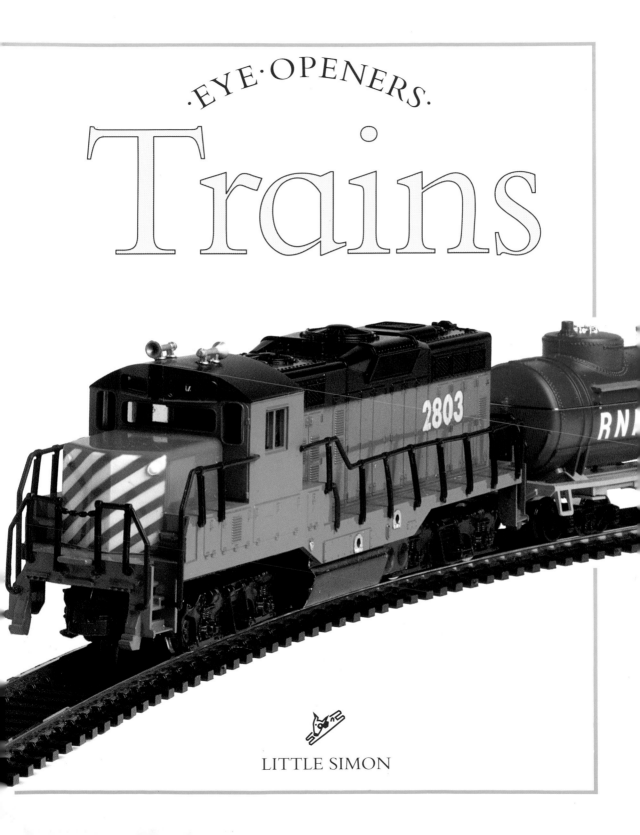

·EYE·OPENERS·
Trains

LITTLE SIMON

Steam engine

This steam engine is very old. The fireman puts coal on the fire to heat the water in the boiler. Steam from the hot water makes the engine go. A loud whistle tells people that the train is coming.

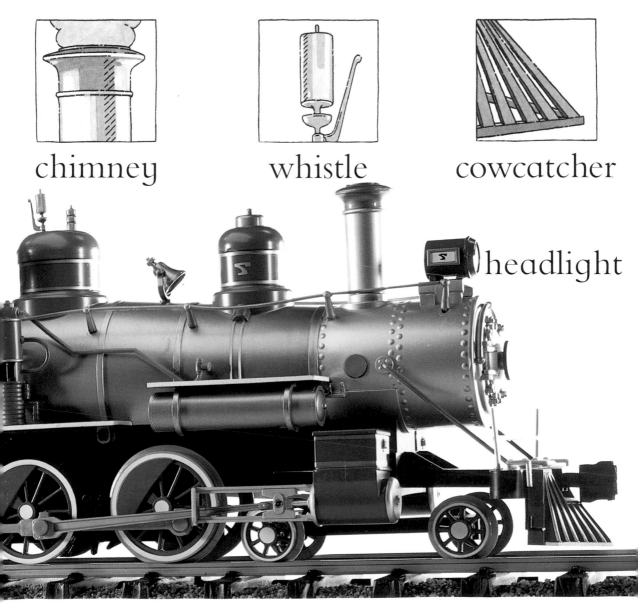

chimney   whistle   cowcatcher

headlight

High-speed train

This train travels very fast. The engine uses electricity from a wire above the track to make it go. The train tilts as it speeds around bends. This makes the ride very smooth for the passengers. They can barely feel that the train is moving.

28

SNCF

pantograph

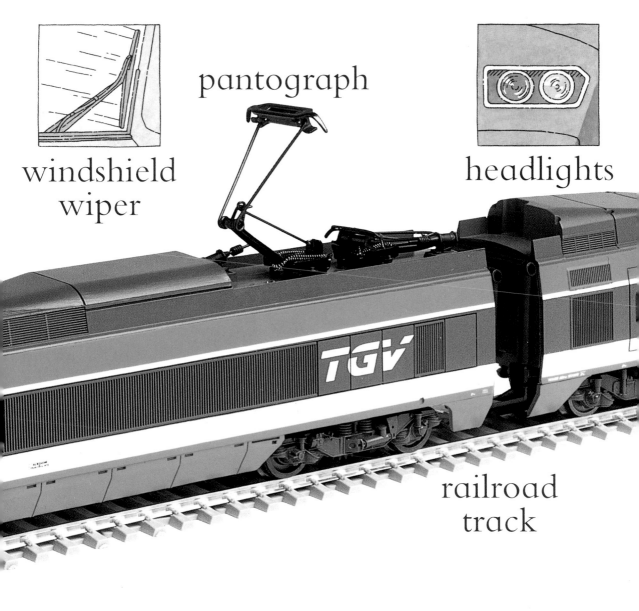

windshield
wiper

headlights

railroad
track

9

Crane train

The crane train clears the railroad track of fallen trees and other heavy things. If a train goes off the track, the crane train is sent to help. It uses its jib and big hook to lift the train car back onto the track.

hook

jib

cab

11

Crocodile train

The crocodile train is
used to pull train cars
up into the mountains.
The long engine bends on
each side. This helps the train
get around the steep, rocky corners.

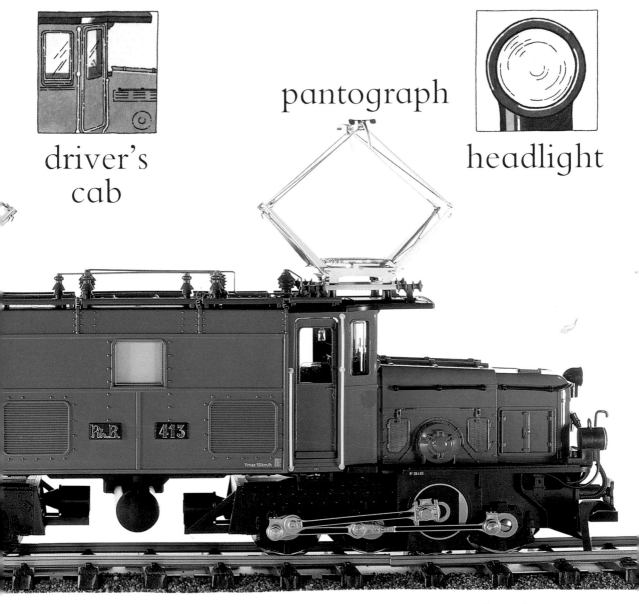

driver's
cab

pantograph

headlight

RhB. 413

Vmax 55km/h

 13

Passenger train

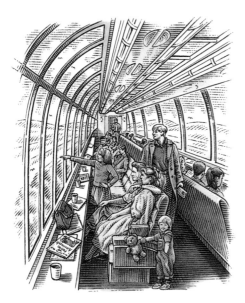

This train uses diesel oil and electricity to make it go. It carries passengers from one place to another. The passengers can sit back and enjoy the view as the train speeds along.

double-decker car

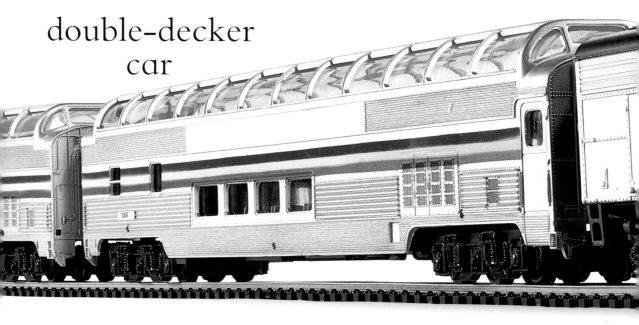

horn

window

cab

15

Freight train

A freight train transports all kinds of heavy loads. Each car carries something different. The tank car carries oil. The caboose is always the last car on the train.

caboose   wheel   ladder

tank
car

box car

Switcher

The switcher is a strong train that works in the railroad yard. It pulls freight train cars across the yard to the unloading site. The switcher also pushes train cars into the sheds at the end of the day.

engine

06 005

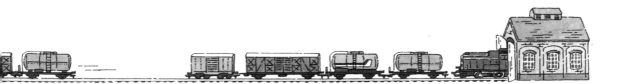

buffer   wheels   window

train car

Orient Express

The Orient Express is a famous old train. It carries people on short holiday trips. Passengers like to travel in its old-fashioned cars. Meals are served in the dining car. And at night, passengers sleep in bunk beds in the sleeper car.

air vent   door   window

sleeper
car

dining car